Prewritten Letters for Your Convenience

By Kansas Bowling & Parker Love Bowling

Cover Artwork by Elizabeth Zamets

www.farwestpress.com
First Edition
978-1-7365388-9-0
Printed in the United States of America

This book is dedicated to those who believed in themselves, took a risk, and turned The Source Restaurant into Cabo Cantina.

Dear Kansas,

Gee whiz. I've always very much enjoyed being your sister.

RIP.

Just kidding! This isn't a eulogy! This is an introduction! What I enjoyed most about growing up with you, was all the games we'd play that evidently, lasted for years. One of these games was of course, our letter writing game. And boy, did we have game. Kansas, why don't you explain to the readers, what our letter writing game was.

Love your little sister,
Parker La Bomlig

Dearest Parker —

Thank you for that warm introduction! I would be glad to fill our readers' in on what exactly we have going on here.

You see, back when I was around 11 and Parker was 8, we began to compile prewritten (by us) "letters" that would eventually fill a book marketed to those who dread letter writing. This book would have every letter you could ever possibly need already written for you!

Obviously the final draft of the book was ∞ pages long, so we've selected some of the best for you.

Please enjoy some of our early yet incredibly advanced humor, and don't be afraid to use any in your every day letter-writing-free lives!

♡ Kansas Bowling

07/10/2021

(866) 908-5220
5582 McFadden Avenue
Huntington Beach, CA 92649

(877) 908-5220
175 S. Lake Avenue #200
Pasadena, CA 91101

Make sure to take out the trash sweetheart. I love you.

Take out the trash.

— Linda

Loopy,

You are the
WORST maid
I've ever hired.
Take out the
trash FOR ONCE!!!

— Ren

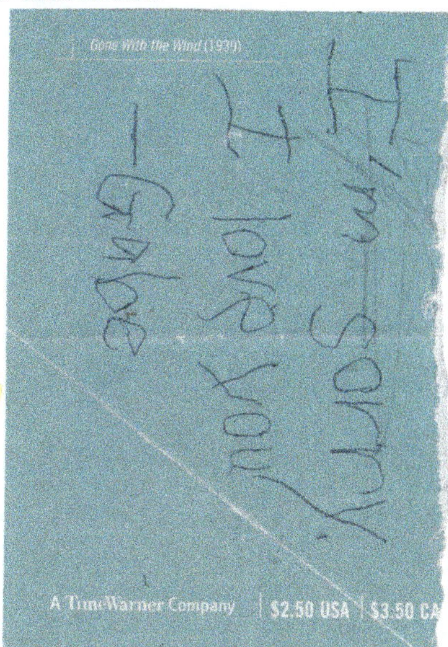

I want a 12
string guitar
just like John
Lennon had.

Momma,
Ashleys shert said this "I'm kind of a big deal." Can I have one too Please? Thank you so much.
Love,
Muffy Anne

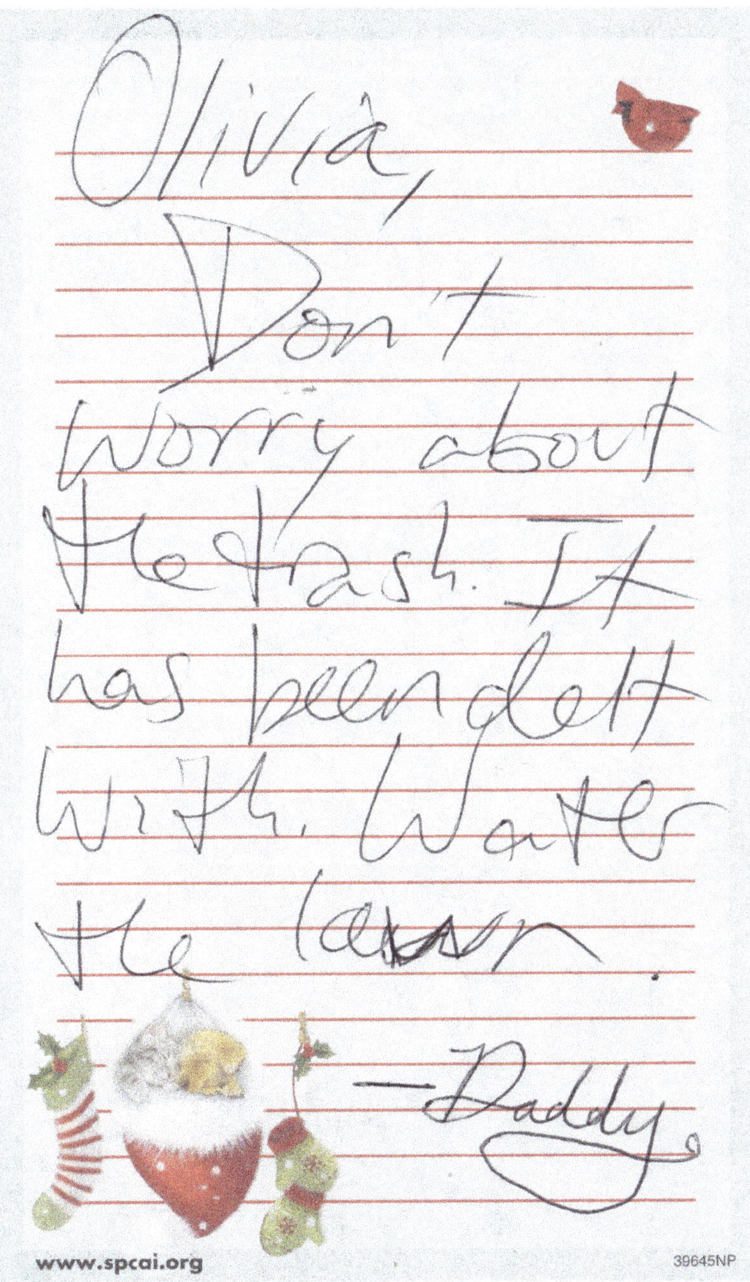

Olivia,

Don't worry about the trash. It has been dealt with. Water the lawn.

—Daddy

I'm going to
work. Take
out the trash.
— Afro
Stan

Don't lift hat.
BIG BUG
UNDERNBATH!
— Kansas

Your face is like a prison.

—Dad.

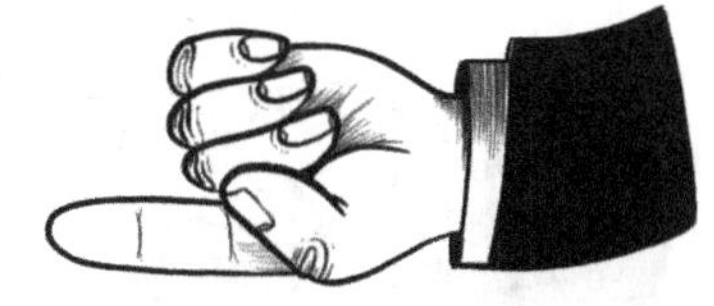

Goodwill

Beverly & Fairfax #30
323-556-0060
7919 BEVERLY BLVD, LOS ANGELES 90048
****
Station # : 3
199753   10/14/2012   13:29:49

Cashier is :   MaSoumeh M

I serve romance.

Qty		Reg.Price		Sub.Tot
1 110G		6.49	0	6.49
	W PANTS			
1 19B		5.99	0	5.99
W TOPS - LONG SLEEVE				

Subtotal   12.48
Total   12.48
VISA   12.48

Refund within 7 days of purchase with
original receipt and tags.
Returns of $100 or more paid by cash,
check, or debit card will be
refunded as a check sent from
the corporate office.

Join us on Facebook and Twitter
www.GoodwillSoCal.org

0303199759

DOUBLE   13   SIDED

P.S.

BITCH

PLEASE!!!

P.S.S. bitch double please!!!
P.S.S.S. bitch triple please!!! etc...

Next time you decide to spend my money you better make damn sure I don't find the receipt
—Big Mac

USA National Title Company

(866) 908-5220
5582 McFadden Avenue
Huntington Beach, CA 92649

(877) 908-5220
175 S. Lake Avenue #200
Pasadena, CA 91101

Hey ya'll! I miss you a ton! Georgia isn't the same without ya' girl!

-Your bestie,

Reyanne!

P.S. That hunk Joey still loves you.

If you feel any sort of pain, boil some sugar and pour it on the wound. Make sure it's steaming hot or else it won't kill life-threatening bacteria. Then, make sure to rub it with baby oil.

Doctor's orders.

—Dr. Oz

Hey Kiddo!

Dinner is on the stove. Green Bean will be home at eight. Try ~~to~~ not to disturb him — work has been tough! I'll be out late (hopefully) ~~because~~ I have my eyes set on that cute Italian gigilo. If you need homework help, call Kato Kaelin.

xoxo
Mama Cassss

Well guess what?
I'm gonna write a NOVEL
about how you always
wanna be on top of me!

Steel Boy,
  Let's go to this. ⟶ (turn over)

We won't regret it.
If you go away...if you go away
...if you go away...

— Piggy Fan

DOUBLE 20 SIDED

TAKE THE TRASH OOUT OF HERE!
But seriously honey, CAN you take out the TRASH?
— NUG n' DUMP

Dear Momo,

I think we should stop seeing each other. I just met a man that I absolutely need to tap, so I cant really have you around during my pursuit. I hope you understand. You probably dont want to hear about him, but his name is Dissel and I hear its 78 in. long. Dont feel bad though, because yours has personality.

Love,
From,
Momo (Ya, thats right. Its me.)

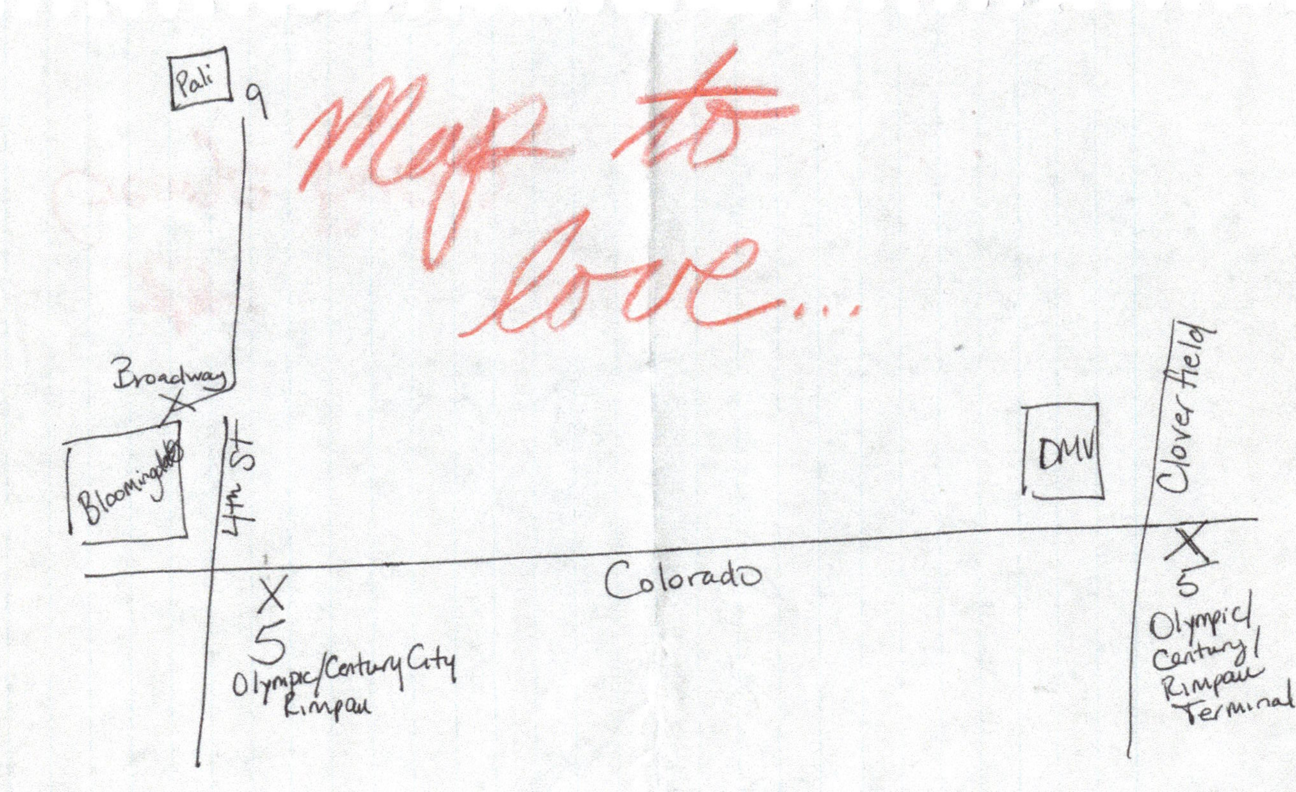
Pali
9
Map to love...
Broadway
4th St
Bloomingdale's
DMV
Cloverfield
Colorado
5
Olympic/Century City
Rimpau
5
Olympic/
Century/
Rimpau
Terminal

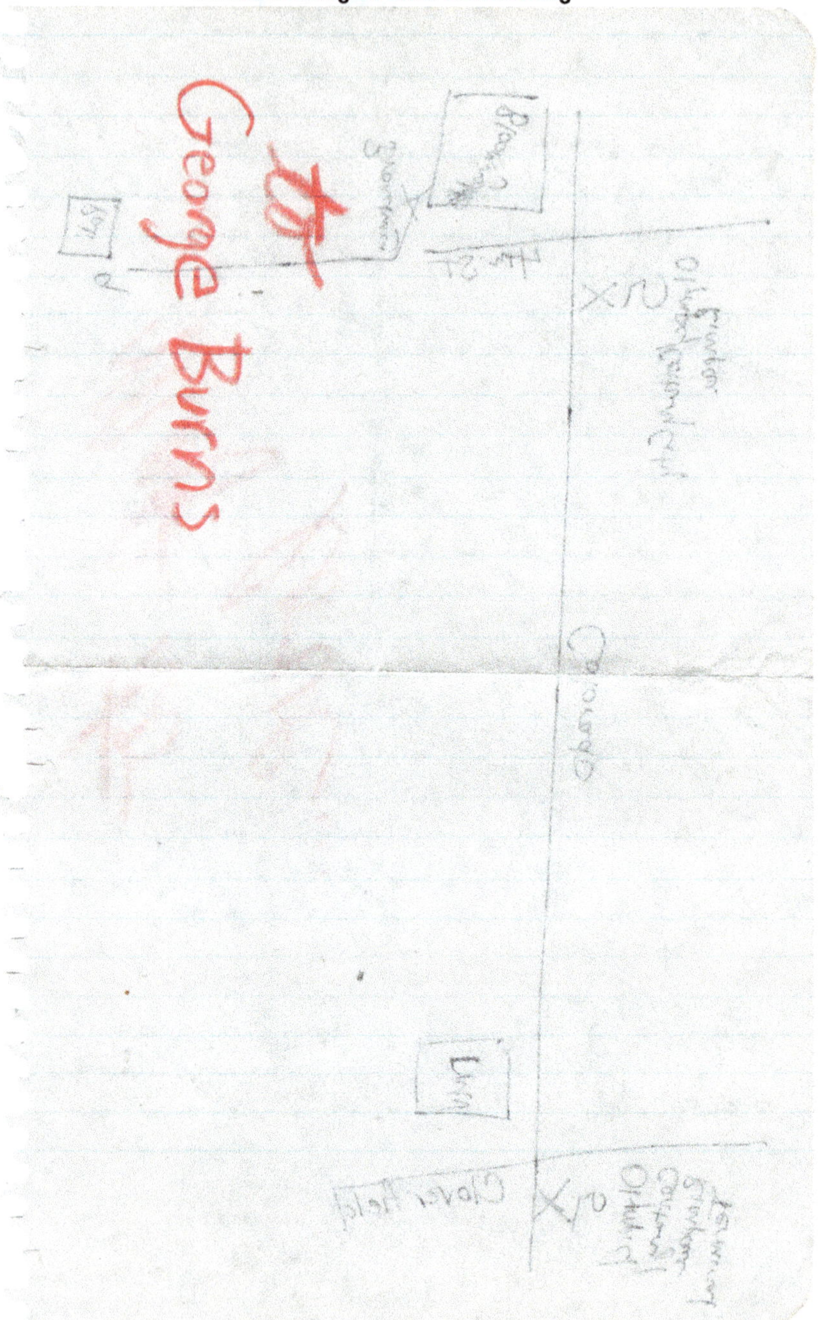
George Burns
Colorado

3/5/11

Dear sketch book,
    Today we are at the park. We are sitting RIGHT next to a Frank Lloyd Wright house and it is sooooo incredible! I feel like I'm in Egypt. Beware of mummies! Ha! Amanda's crazy mind says it looks like an Egyptian tomb. Yikes! I hope I don't turn into mummy stew! Well, I have to go. My _annoying_ sister wants me to take a nap with her. She still can't fall asleep without me after all these years. Then my mom's making me write an educational essay about all I've learned today. See Ya!

                — Jules
P.S. I cannot wait until I get a goldfish. I'll name it Michelle Pfieffer.

Dear Mrs. Toxie,

"IMAGINATION"
by Chuck Chang
pen and marker
on paper
2003-2004

Do you think I have what it takes to be in your advanced art class? Let me know. Thanks.

Chuck Chang

P.S. This is just a quick sketch. Imagine what I could do if I really put my mind to it. Really used my... IMAGINATION...

~~Dear Mr. President,~~
Dear Johnny Hold-Up,

I am having a lot of trouble without you here. I really miss you. And trust me - I hate to admit it. I know I kicked you out. I know it. I'm guilty. I'm sorry. But I was wrong. I know you've probably already moved on and had plenty of affairs, but listen up buster, that's not the case for me. It is hard to believe, yes - I know that Uncle Jesse, _the_ Uncle Jesse, hasn't been laid since you left but it is the sad truth. And not only that, but I don't even find anyone attractive anymore. Hold-Up, nobody seems real compared to you.

There's something else I've been meaning to tell you, Hold-Up. I've been having these dreams You're in them. And so is that midget from "Willow". I know it's not that weird so far since Willow is your favorite movie, but it gets worse. The Willow midget starts undressing you. And you just let him. And I am watching in terror and trying to stop it but I have a silent scream and frozen muscles. Then you are completely naked and the willow midget starts licking you. But it's really gentle. Like the way a cat would lick you. And come to think of it, his tongue was small and delicate like a cat's. This goes on for a long time until he licks every area on your body. And you are sitting there smiling. I have calmed down by now but my heart is still racing. Your whole body has a glossy layer now and light is reflecting off of it. But the light gets brighter and brighter. I try to scream again but I can't. It's like my vocal cords have been snipped.

Soon, the light is so bright that I have to close my eyes. So I do. What I see with my eyes closed is just white. The brightest white you could imagine. Then, I begin ~~to~~ to feel little hands touch my body. The willow midget's hands. At first I try to resist it, to squirm, but I am so relaxed all of the sudden. It's as if these hands have put a spell on me. He's feeling my body. Feeling it everywhere. And then I feel something cold touch my neck. It's metal. And then it clamps around my neck. I hear a chain rattle. He locked me to this necklorace. Then, the white fades away and I can open my eyes. You two are standing in front of me with menacing grins. You two are physically separate, but I know that mentally you are now one. Slowly, you creep toward me in unision and start licking me. Your tongue is now like his. Except when it actually happens, it is not calming but painful. Your tongues feel sharp and sticky. My skin becomes raw. Then, for the rest of the dream you two take turns raping me. It is so awful Hold-Up.

    I've actually never had that dream but I keep thinking how awful it would be if I actually did. Please come back so I don't have to have it. I'm not trying to make you feel guilty or anything, but please do. Please.

          — Uncle Jesse
          (Yes, _the_ Uncle Jesse.)

doodie

—your boyfriend

Don't tell
S.S.

I wish you'd
learn to keep
your mouth shut!
—Hessee

My dearest pen pal Athur,

Wow! I didn't expect you to be that handsome! Well, I attached my photo. I'm not as atractive as you, but I'm not too bad. I'm saving up all my pennys so I can sea you Athur. But every night I just look at the stars and think of you face. If only you had a face star so I could look at the stars AND you're face. Hurry up technology! Oh well, Bill gates will come up with it one day. How are things with you? Are your grades improving? Your sooo smart. ♥ I'm naked.

Love

Samanta Bingo

Son,

I gave this to you
because I think you
should go. I'm 76.6%
sure that you are gay,
so show some pride and
get out there sonny!
Go out there and make
yo' old man proud!

With waaaaay too
much love,
Pops' (me)

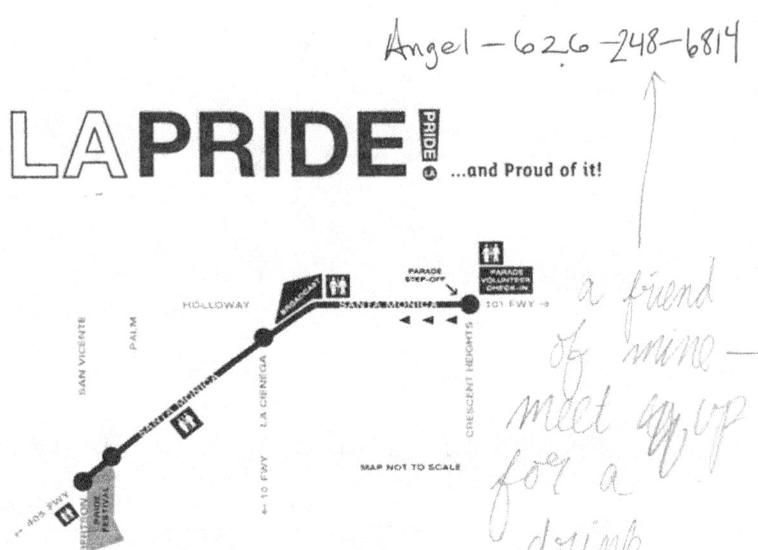

Angel — 626 248-6814

a friend of mine — meet up for a drink

Time & Route
Where do you run in to thousands of your nearest and dearest in Los Angeles? At the annual LA PRIDE Parade, set to step off this year on **Sunday, June 10, at 11:00 a.m. Attendees should plan to arrive early (about 10:30am). The Macy's/Bloomingdale's teams gather at the red Macy's balloon. Look for this balloon at Norton (which is off of Crescent Heights, North of Santa Monica).**

Traffic will be closed on Santa Monica Blvd. between Fairfax Ave. and Doheny Dr. starting at 6:00 a.m. on Sunday, June 10. Santa Monica Blvd. will re-open immediately at the end of the end of the Parade, which may be as late as 4:00 p.m.

Parking
Parking and traffic congestion on Parade day in West Hollywood is impossible at best; any vehicles parked illegally will be towed away. Suggested parking areas include East of Fairfax, Pacific Design Center, the Kings Road parking structure, and the Beverly Center. **Parking permits in West Hollywood are waived from 7:00 a.m. Saturday to 7:00 a.m. Monday.**

USA
National Title Company
(866) 908-5220
5582 McFadden Avenue
Huntington Beach, CA 92649
(877) 908-5220
175 S. Lake Avenue #200
Pasadena, CA 91101

don't tempt me
bitch

Take out the trash or die.
— Uncle Jesse ♥

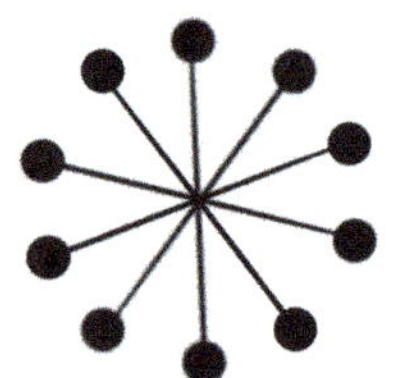

I don't want to say it anymore. Take out the fucking trash. — Lucy Florence

Fiona Chen of Fiona Chen Events —

If you make my party seem — in any way ASIAN, I will not only fire you, but I will put my dog's shock collar on you. I hope you recieve this message loud and clear.

Your client

ZenBen

I can't see you. You're in black and white. There's no color between us. I miss our spark Our fire and desire. When will our romance come back. We have been married for 29 years, I don't want that 29th year to be our last.

Love,
Your wife (Not for long I won't be. That's the way you want it.)

← woops, sorry I spilt my <u>black</u> as night coffee mixed with Jack Daniels on the paper

Dear lead singer from Black Veil Brides,

You have really nice hair, do you cut it yourself? I cut my hair but it looks professional. It doesn't look very pretenshous, and I have a beautiful voice. I'm gonna draw you (on →) (back) really nice even though I'm not gonna try; 3 minutes <u>MAX.</u> My name is KayKay, but people usually call me <u>KEGZ</u> because my last name starts with a Z. I'm really unique. I think I've died my hair just about every color in the book, and I read <u>ALOT</u> of books, like this one guy you probably never heard of unless you're into the whole underground thing. His name is Albert Camus. And I so love Animal Farm because of communism or something and because I'm Russian, like, 3/4. I am so tired and I'm on the phone with my boyfriend while I'm writing this letter. There are like 30 seniors trying to have sex with me, but I close him through via email.

KEEERZ
ME <3333
You as a
tortured black raven
with a Broken
WING
If you write me back, I'll send you a glue made of beads.
YOUR NAME HERE
(I'm crafty.)

Just forgive me.
Just forgive me.

— Gabe

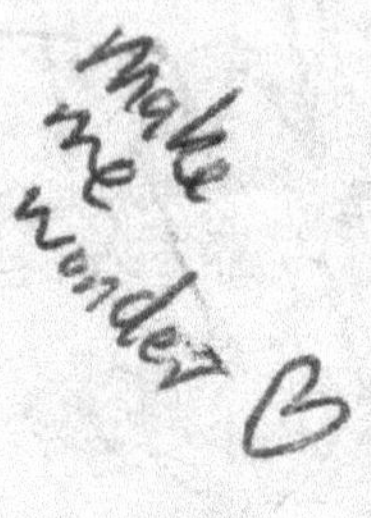

Dear Maid Julie,
You forgot to scrub between all the tiles again!! & looks like someone likes sleeping in the tool shed

Sincerely,
The future Parker Love Bowling

Dear mom,

John Denver visited me in my dreams again last night. This time it wasn't so great. He's usually so jovial, but here, he was just... sad. Oh, I couldn't take it. I just needed to wrap my arms around him and tell him things would be alright. But he looked at me and said, "Take me home country roads to the place I found a frog." I was confused because those weren't the lyrics, but I suddenly realized what he meant. He showed me a photograph of him as a boy. He was ~~in~~ the country holding a frog. But when I looked closer, I realized.... the boy was me... Then, John Denver melted into a pile of mashed potatoes and I woke up. Mommy, I'm scared.

— Jeff the Chef

Jessica,

if you're looking for a good time, call my baby brother, Jack. He's only 8, but really naughty :)

— annie

To OldYeller

Dear Old Yeller,
    I am 6 years old. I am a fan of you. When will you come to Wisconsin? I will wait for you and then we can play.
    My name is Alan. Call me Al.

Love,

ALAN

21

PRIES✝ING 101

Dress code:
Besides the usual (robe and all), we priests need to follow a simple rule to staying presentable: We need to wear keens,* stay clean, and smell of chlorine. Heres an easier way to remember it: KKK

① K — KEEN
② K — KLEAN
③ K — KLORINE

See? Its easy! You're almost a priest!

*Crocs are acceptable only on Catholic holidays and only if they are accompanied by Catholic themed Croc accessories.
(For KKK, replace KEEN with KROCS.)

. . . . Priest chic!

Dear Preezy of the United Steezy,
    I don't like the way things are run
around here!

    Fix it!

    — Angry American

I'm going off the grid if you keep it up!

To Olivia
Love Goldie

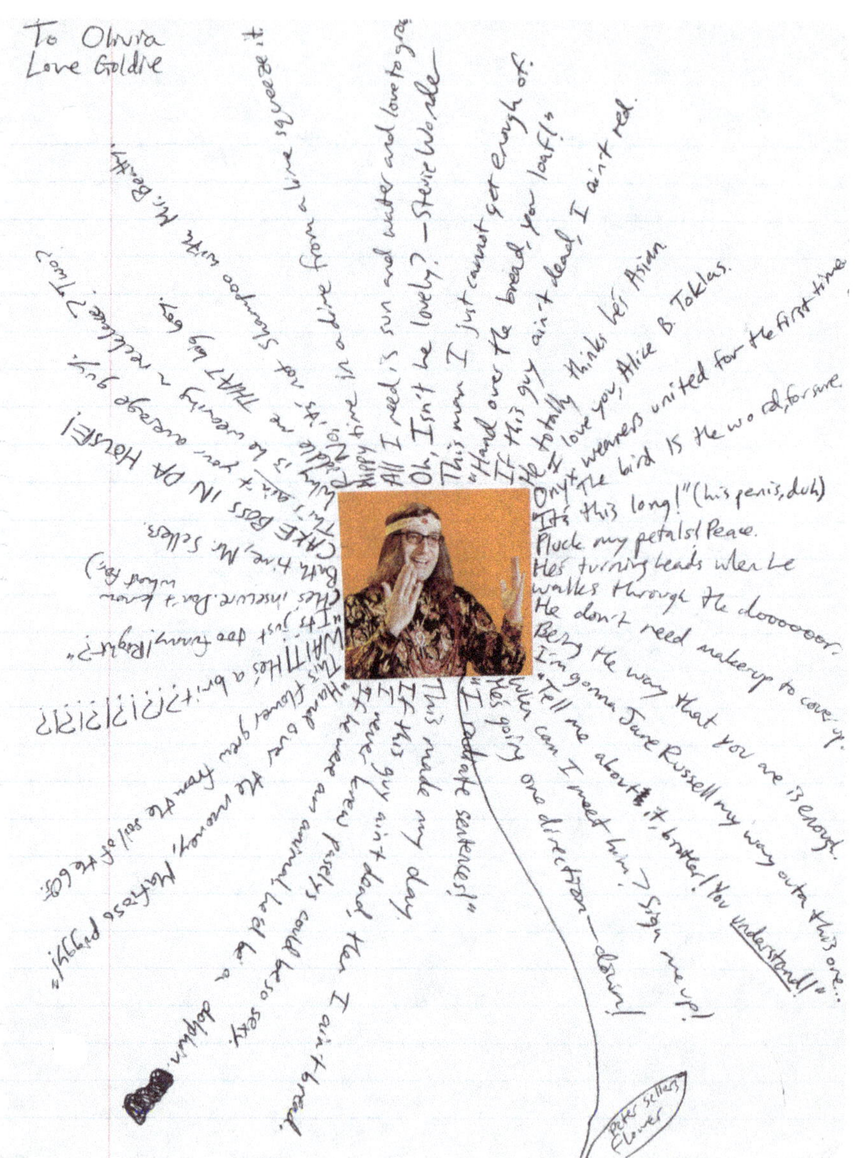

Happy time in a lime from a lime squeeze it.
All I need is sun and water and love to grow.
Oh, Isn't he lovely? —Stevie Wonder
This man, I just cannot get enough of.
"Hand over the bread, you loaf!"
If this guy ain't dead, I ain't red.
He totally thinks he's Asian
I love you, Alice B. Toklas.
Onyx wearers united for the first time
The bird IS the word, for sure.
It's this long!" (his penis, duh)
Pluck my petals! Peace.
He's turning heads when he walks through the dooooooor.
He don't need makeup to cover up.
Being the way that you are is enough.
I'm gonna Jane Russell my way outta this one...
Tell me about it, brother! You understand!"
When can I meet him? Sign me up!
He's going one direction—down!
"I radiate sentences!"
This made my day.
If this guy ain't dead, I ain't red.
I never knew her. I ain't bread.
If he were an animal he'd be a dolphin.
"He's a flower grew from the memory, Ms. Piggy!
This flower grew from the memory. Meatless could be a... sell at $6.69!"
"WAIT! He's a bit...
"It's just dee funny. Right?"
He's insecure. Don't know what to...
¿?¿?¿?¿?¿?¿?¿?
But 4 me, Mr. Sellers.
(Gay Porn)
CAKE BOSS IN DA HOUSE!
This ain't your average guy.
THAT by by
Reddie is to woonity to be your average guy
Shampoo with Mr. Beatty!

ALAIN DOBIN
323-555-6465
dobeisgreat.actor@yahoo.com

EDUCATION

West Covina Elementary Acting Camp / 1983

THEATRE

Bye Bye Birdie ... Fan   West Covina Elem.
Willy Wonka ... Oompa Loompa   West Covina Elem.

TELEVISION

Wheel of Fortune ... Contestant
90210 ... Featured Extra

FILM

Bloodsucking Vampires Vs. Vegans ... Vegan

SPECIAL SKILLS

Nunchucks, can hold breath for 106 seconds straight, ambidextrous, clean, really smart, Microsoft Word

FINGER
PRINT

Alain Dobin

DOUBLE 50 SIDED

Amy baby ———

When I see you working so hard all day for that small money, babe it really hurts my heart. Hits me BAM right in the chest. So how bout I save you all the trouble of earning your living and you can just be my baby. Huh? How does it sound sweetie pie? I'll even buy you sweet things and spoil you rotten pretty hun. Quit messing around with all this childish "stem-cell research" you've been doing, cause you know it'll get you no where, hun. I'd say you, me, and my Redondo Beach condo sounds like heaven on earth compared to what you have going for you now.

So, whatd ya say?

Hit me up pretty honey,

— Sack

Dear Mr. Hennenkicker,

    It has come to my attention that you are teaching "evolution" in your science class. Now, I am not religious, nor am I opposed to your teachings. What does concern me though is that my son Franklin is very sensitive to certain material. This includes cotton, silk, and any type of polyester. Also, he's afraid of monkeys, if you want to get relevant. So is there a way you can phrase all of the evolution talk in a way that makes it seem like we did <u>NOT</u> come from monkeys? I think it'd be better for all of us. Preferrably, I'd like you to teach your students we were birthed from volcanoes and that we're all made of ash. But I'm sure you can figure something out.

    One grateful
      parent,

Roxanne Gibbons

To whomever Oriental man this may concern!

WARNING.

I'm really depressed. I need someone to talk to. I'm in a dump. Literally. Not a dumpy place but like... a dump. Where trash is. I found some dirty toilet paper and banana peels. I came here because in movies people go to the dump and find all those interesting things. So I come and I find shit. Well, that's life for you. Ching chong China. Bye.

X ________________

(Miguel and Matthew and Waverly the talking fish)

Bonnie / stop being a bitch. You upset me eternally.

Sincerely,

Gary Oldman

Don't you
even dare
cross me
Take out the
Trash.
Bitch please —
Angie

"Cheap Detective"
by Marcus Knight
FIRST DRAFT
(don't judge lol)

Fade in. We see a hooded man with a pipe and a Sherlock Holmes hat and a large magnifying glass. He is a spy, but you can't tell. A man approaches him looking nervous.

MAN
He-Hey. You buyin' right? I need to make this quick—no fuzz, detectives involved, see?

SPY
No spies here. (Looks at camera, winks)

MAN
Kay, here's the dime bag. (whispers) Cocaine. Now

Let's exchange. Moola, por favor.

SPY

Can you break a $20?

MAN

Huh?

The spy takes the cocaine and pours it into his cupped hand as the drug dealer watches. He then blows it all into his face leaving him stunned.

SPY

How's that for a laugh...?

MAN

Wh-wh-why??????????
F-f-f-fuzz!!!

The man tries to run but the spy grabs him by his underwear and the elastic makes him swing back right into the spy's open palm.

SPANK!

I'll bet you like girls that WIGGLE? Don't you? you SICK freak. freak of nature. freak of society. Circus freak. Circus geek. Geek squad / Fucking sicko. —ZORRO

When is this fucking trash going to be taken out? It smells a is rotting. I can't do it because I don't have hands.

— Terry Jacks

USA

National Title Company

(866) 908-5220

5582 McFadden Avenue
Huntington Beach, CA 92649

(877) 908-5220

175 S. Lake Avenue #200
Pasadena, CA 91101

This is a warning.
For Real! Next time I'll
notefy the popo. You
better watch your back

— Your neighbors
Dan Trout.

Ok Jeff ——

Stay the fuck away from CeeCee. I know she's a grown up and she can fend for herself, but I feel I have to stand up for her this time. I never imagined I'd hear about you having one of your "public golden shower episodes" AGAIN — but there you went. If you piss on CeeCee in public one more time, I swear, I'll have your nuts in my hand in an extremely violent way. Save the apologies for a sucker because this tough chickey can see through your bullshit, you pissing perv.

Take my word — Stay away

Danny Bonaduce

I love you
Lilly

Love your
mother,
Angie

I love you honey!

Love,

Angie

I love you honey!

Love,

Angie

DEAR FBI,
   I HAVE SUCH A MAJOR CRUSH ON YOU. YOU DON'T EVEN KNOW. DON'T KILL ME, BUT I KNOW ALL OF YOUR SECRETS! KISSES!

— JENNY ☆

P.S. CAN YOU SEND ME A PICTURE? AFTER ALL THESE YEARS I STILL DON'T KNOW WHAT YOU LOOK LIKE. I BET YOU'RE HUNKY, WITH SANDY BLONDE HAIR. SOME-DAY I'LL PEEP AT YOUR ROCKIN BOD. OR AT LEAST A PHO—TAW—GRAPH.

To Dracula, aka Bill Bowling

You know I love you and I always will. I wish I went to that concert with you many years back.

Love,
Mira aka Winona Ryder

please honey, be a doll and take out the trash.

love
dracula

P.S. Bitch Please

Come over after school. I got sum I wanna show. :)

Uh-oh. What??

My dick.

How did I know? I always say your smart.

Thx! :)

If I show will you show?

Hmmm...maybe? :)

Yessss.

Your so funny!

DRAWING oh hey

Gwenith Palthrow

you pperv.

you know me.

im me.

wow omg funny

No your funny

No you

funny

No you

Dear Edith and
George, ♡
Get out
of my
house. Mow
the lawn first.
Bye!
— Janet

Dearest Nina,

I have been staying at Morris, Forks, for a little over three, whole days. I cannot stop my mind from thinking about you - even in the midst of battle! The image of your lovely buttox comes to my mind, even when death faces me. I cannot wait to come home and enjoy some nice apple crumble by the fire. Oh Nina if you weren't so sweet, you'd make sugar taste just like salt! These woods we are staying in are so dark and deep. It can only remind me of those nights when we would go out in the rain and flatten all of the faeries homes so they'd have time to leave before their houses flooded. We saved hundreds of little guys that night and what did we get out of it? Nothing. Thats what I love you! You do things for other people. You are so incredibly kind. You make me marvel! How are you so amazing!? I am truly flabberghasted. Well, when I get back, lets all go down to his gentelmen's club again. This time lets bring Kacey and the rest of the girls and have a fun night out! I'm looking at our tatoo right now. Its making me want a hamburger so terribly. I haven't had one in years! Well I'm probably boring you. Its just that I could write for hours. Its the only fun I could have out here. I just miss you so damn much. Oh no. Leutnant Lee is coming, I better hide you somewhere) Lt. Lee doesn't appriciate us writing. He says it distracts us from our duties for our country. Oh no! He saw you! Lt. Lee! Stop! Stop right now! No! No! No!

THIS IS LT. LEE. I'M GONNA KILL YOU LIKE I DID YOUR LOVER. THAT'S HIS BLOOD. I'D SAVOR IT BECAUSE YOU AIN'T GETTING ANYTHING ELSE FROM HIM. HE AIN'T COMING HOME.

BUT I LOVE YOU NINA. MAYBE WE CAN WORK THIS OUT NOW

HERE'S MY NUMBER.

213-304-4307

CALL ME

Six fingers v.s. fists for hands   7-15-133
CHAFT
is one baaaaad BOY.
v.s.
Kurt Hustle
Both wear hoens and fedoras! Double Trouble!
He's steaming mad AND super bad!
Battle between Evil and Evil!

2

Kurt Hustle:

Kurt Hustle and Kurt Russel were from the same womb, at the same time. (Twins) A birth defect caused them both to have very small eyes and thick necks. While Kurt Russel decided to not dwell on that and moved onto acting, Kurt Hussel did everything he could do to enlarge his eyes and shrink his fat neck. Through these various attempts, Kurt Hussel caused himself permanent sores around his neck and dark scars around his eyes. Most of these various methods included potions, which have had terrible side effects, including fur growing on his legs, beans sprouting from his feet, a fedora forever attached to his scalp, hands clenched into fists, and a terrible stench to follow him wherever he goes. While Kurt Russel enjoys fame, Kurt Hussel lives a life of embarrassment and ridicule from that...

(At least he has Kurt Russels beautiful, flowy hair.)

Dear Haruki Murakami,

You are so weird! I don't know how you diggity do it! It's all like how do you think of this crazy stuff? I mean, I know you're Asian and all. Do Asian people think like you? I wouldn't know. I'm white. But of Danish decent. You know, strong cheekbones and <u>all</u>.

But really, a man talks to cats in <u>Kafka on the Shore</u>. CATS. Did you know that that is impossible? I tried it, but nothing happened. The cat just saw my figgity face and was all like.... Whaaa? White girl???? Maybe I should be Asian. Is that the trick. Do you do it? Oh look at me. I figured it out. My mom always told me I was smart. But I never believed her until now.

Sometimes your books can be a little innappropriate though. It's ok. I'm 19 so I know all about the birds and the bees. But it can get a little awkward reading about erections if you're a girl. Because I have a vagina. I don't know about that stuff. Unless you're talking about goldfish.

So I was wondering if you were single. I am really interested. I really pretty and smart but you know that by now. If you are interested just write me back. Tell me.

What was your childhood like?
Right now I'm baking baked Alaska. I've always wondered why they called it that since you don't bake it. I added some pineapple this time. Do you like pineapple? It's kind of a must for me. Right now the cake is all mushy and moist and warm. What does that remind you of, babe? It's not an erection, I'll tell you that much. :

So since you're an author and all I bet you like books. My favorite author is Hercule Poirot. He writes these stories about murders he solves. He's really smart. You should check him out sometime. They can get a little confusing though, just to warn you. He's always talking in olde English/he says little Brit idioms like "apple pie in the eye" and "cheerios". I don't think they have cereal there so that's probably why.

♡LOVE♡ you,
Raquel from Florida
#14 Volleyball Muskrats! WooT!

DON! DON! DON! DON! DON! DON! DON!
Sorry, but I've been doing this thing lately where I write letters to people when I'm bored. And now it's your turn, Don! Plus, it's nice just to check in with people. Especially on lonely nights such as this. I am currently staying at my friends house, but she's away for a week. Well, I shouldn't call it a house. She rents out a renovated tool shed from this sweet old couple for only $550 a month! Can you believe it! It's real a steal. So I'm her roommate. We split all other expenses besides the rent like movie tickets, gas, electric, and prostitutes. It's also really lonely tonight because of the rain. And since this is a toolshed and since it is made of metal it is fucking loud and cold in here I wouldn't be suprized if it was hailing outside. It's actually probably snowing considering there are little frosty bits forming on my eyelashes. Feely I just looked in the mirror and my lips are purple. I might call an ambulence. This looks serious. Oh wait! Duh! God, I'm such a fucking idiot. I can just put on a jacket. Ha! Don, if you can't tell by now, I'm really slow sometimes. Well, I can't imagine you're that interested in what I'm doing tonight, or any night for that matter, considering you

have no idea who I am and I have no idea who you are and that I just picked up an address book I saw a lady drop, ripped out a few pages, returned the book to her, and have been writing to all of the entries. Don't hate me, but I love you. I don't think we should go on like this though.

Formally —

Jimmy Jazz

(Just kidding. I'm just a huge punkrocker.)

Anarchy —

Sheena Ramone

(Seriously, that's my name.)

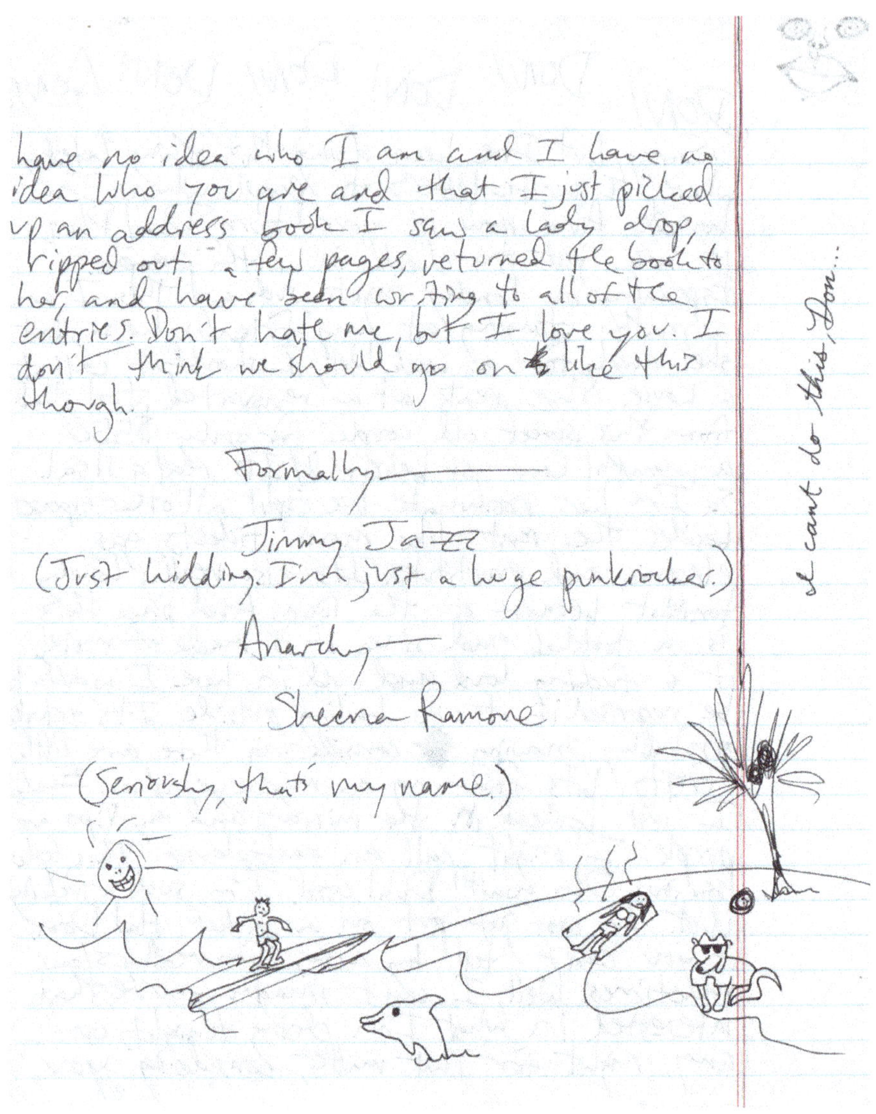

can I have your heart? I need it for science class. Oh wait. You don't have one you horrid bitch. I remembered that because every time I needed a heart, you would always be like, "Get your own." So you don't have one but you need one. Lucy is undead. You should know that by now you fucking idiot. Why is Tom Waits hardly in Dracula? Oh shit. The grave is empty. Where is she? well anyways, enough about dracula. Let's talk more about me. I am very interesting. I've never dropped a baby in my entire life. Except for those two times. Sometimes, when no one is looking, I like to throw up blood. But then I have to clean it up really fast; I began to get gray hair when I was six months old so it was nice talking to you again. I won't ask you for your heart again. I promise. I'll remember.

    Love,
      Your one and only

P.S. Remember your teddy bear shirt? Well, I burned it.

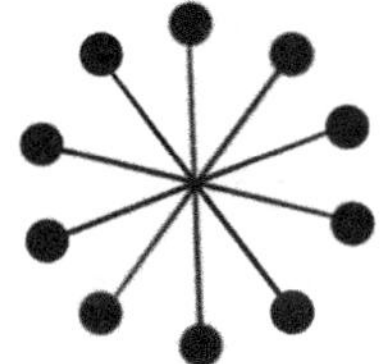

Fido —

Who said dogs couldn't have fun? Ha! Gotta love it!

    — Ivo & Ilan

Dear Kirby,

It is that time of the year where all of us parents must get together and plan an event for our children and to fundraise money for the school. I was thinking something along the lines of a tea party or a George Burns sing-a-long. Give me your thoughts.

Ta-Ta!

—Deborah Silbar

I went all the way to Hot Topic to get the new KROQ STICKER!!! Ahhhh!!!! Sooooooo EXCITED!!!

— Roquel

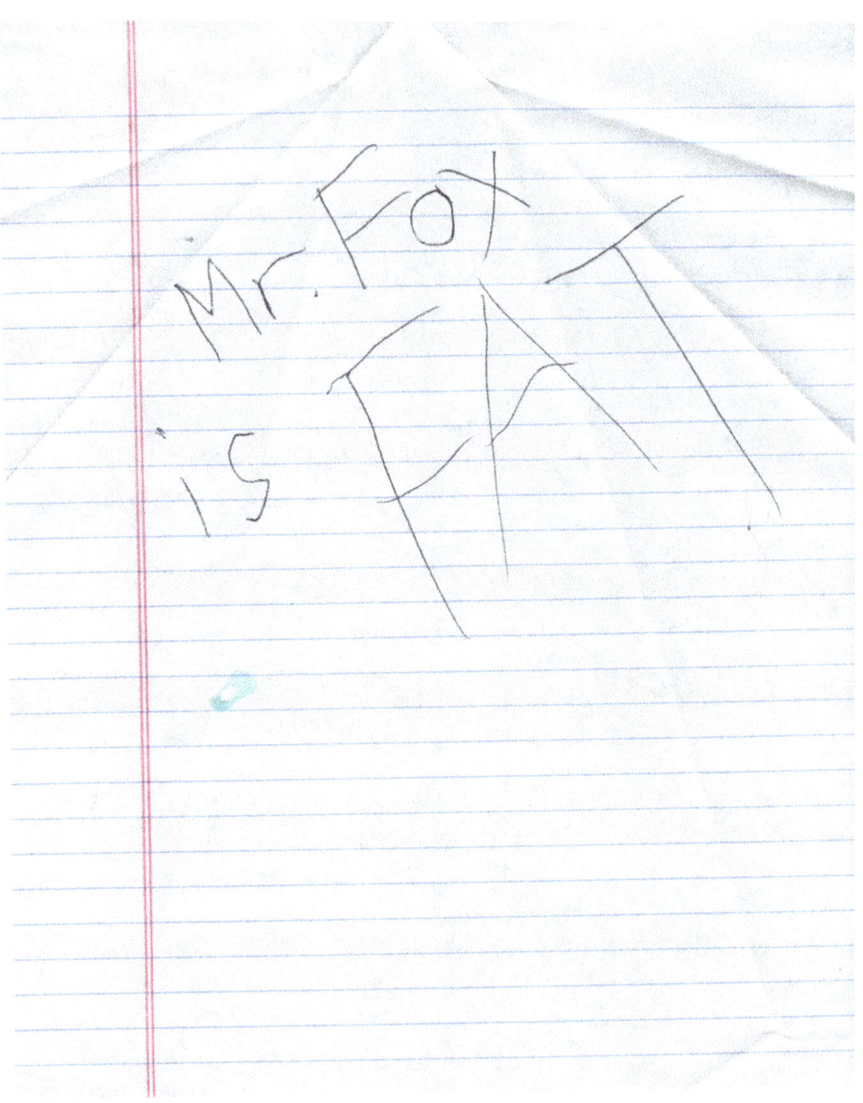
Mr. Fox
is
FAT

I'm gonna kill that fucking dog.

— Anonymous

YOU ATE ALL MY CANOLIS?

HOW DARE YOU!

yum!

5

Fan Fic: "CABO CANDY"

Jane Roberts flopped down on the king size bed in the hotel room. It was temperedic — thank God. The wedding with Braden was beautiful and Braden was so relieved when Jesse showed up to be his best man.

The plane ride was a disaster. A private jet — puhlease. It was more like a kennel but ~~so~~ ~~much~~ after a few long hours, Jane and Braden safely arrived in Cabo. It was Braden's dream honeymoon, since he was such a big fan of Cabo Cantina.

Suddenly, Braden comes out of the bathroom, interrupting Jane's thoughts.

"How do you like it here sweetie?" Jane asked.

"I like it, but it lacks that authenticity that I love so much about Cabo Cantina," Braden replied. "I wish we could've had our honeymoon there."

"I know, babe, but we both desparately needed a break from Hollywood. Don't deny that."

"Oh, no denying that!" Braden said with much enthusiasm. "That town is so suffocating. It'll be the death of me."

"I've never met anybody as anti-Hollywood as you, Braden" Jane said looking at Braden. Her eyes were sparkling. Braden and her were really in love.

Braden lies down next to Jane. His shirt is off revealing his toned belly. He begins to caress Jane's shoulder with his lips.

"Shall we get this honeymoon started, or what?" Jane asked.

"Oh, Jane" Braden said, "I thought you'd never ask."

To Be Continued ← drawn by L.C.

Burrito,

Give me a pot of gold and consider me sold. No one has told me a thing. But for your own safety, consider leaving me a key. No break-ins means no break-outs and no break-outs means no trouble and no trouble means no more rumbles. Because I'm a rumble fish. They nicely named me Pony-Pig.

—Alvin

Angie,

You've been a very good girl this week. Please except this $5.00.

Love your mother,

DRACULA

Some like ME

hot.

— Flame Boy

Dear Alfie,

It's pretty fucking nippy in Vermont right now. I'm dying for a sip of cocoa, but my nutritionist forbids it. Life's fucking tough if you wanna make it big. A big-time tailor, I mean. But these days, there's just so much damn competition. I've seen Japan and I've seen France. I've seen your underpants. But still, nothing compares to Ohio. Maybe I'll move there. I hear they're having a tailor shortage. It's kind of a crisis. And it won't be so fucking nippy. See you in March.

— Graham

Nash '73

(I just put too much soul into all I do...)

Valerie—
I love our bodies and how they connect
I love your sweet breath on my neck

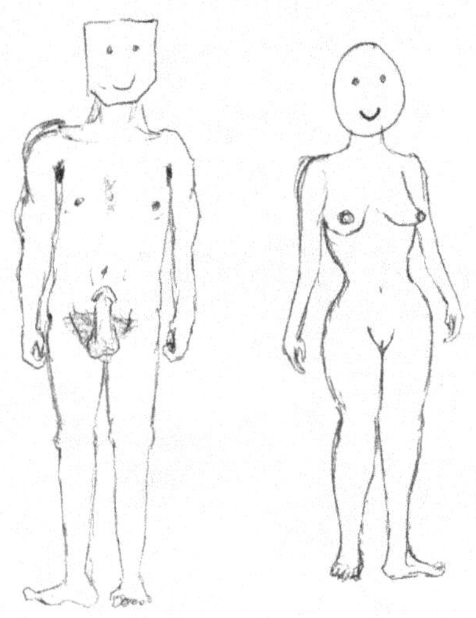

I want your anatomy hanging on my wall
I'll frame it and hang it in my hall

— Tony

Here's a poem for you, my sweet.

You breathe on my neck like a sausage
    breathing on its pray.
Thank you for that.
We are animalistic. Like the Green
    Bear fashion show.
Or was it Seymour?
Who keeps track.
I don't.
I only keep track of your
    breath on my neck.

I wrote that all by myself.
My teacher didn't even proofread
it. Aren't you proud grampy?
I love you. I can't wait until
we get to listen to George Burns
together again. I guess I'll
have to wait until I go to heaven
I guess. Bye!
    —Timmy

Well there it is. My
X-Ray. It's all true
babe. My hands contain
the gift of light and
believe me— I'm NOT
pleased with the news
either. Why can't God
just leave me alone.
Heat up the potatoes.
    —James
    Christ

Dear Mr. Grave Cleaner,
Don't remove this
letter to grampy.

— Timmy

P.S. Bitch Please!

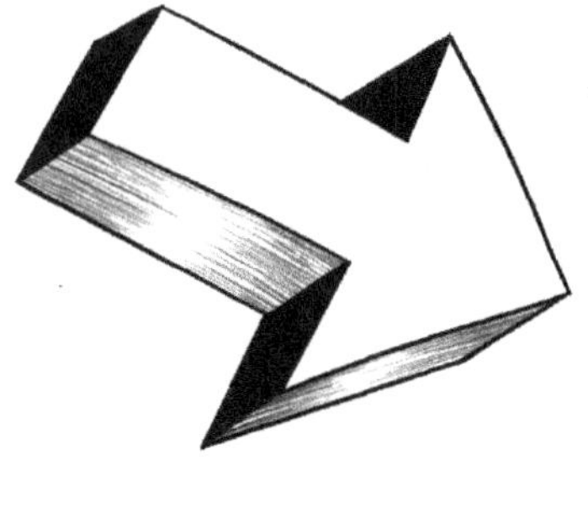

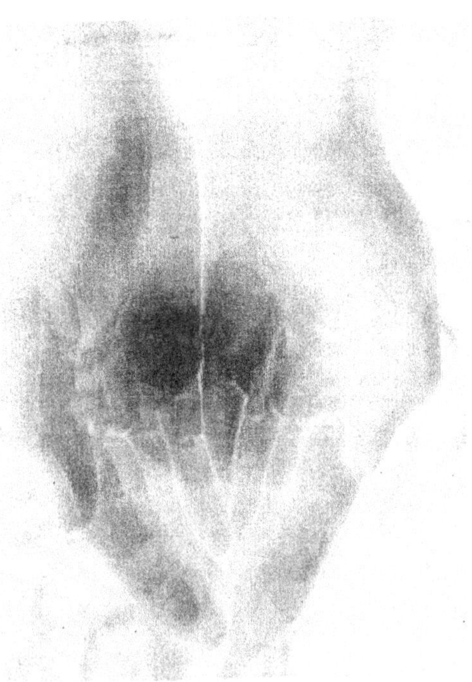

National Title Company

(866) 908-5220
5582 McFadden Avenue
Huntington Beach, CA 92649

(877) 908-5220
175 S. Lake Avenue #200
Pasadena, CA 91101

"Superior Customer Service Without Compromise"
www.usanationaltitle.com

Gagosian New York
I hope you like my drawing. It's an original Toby Bayer piece.

I wouldn't mind if you hung it up, but just give me a cut of profits. Start it at $250,000 in euro. (It's much more posh.)
— Toby Bayer & Assos.

for the pres.
eyes only

<u>Dear future me</u>

I write this time capsule so I can prove everyone wrong. When I/you open this, I WILL be a president!!!!!!!!!! And I have one thing to say— TOLD YA SO!!! —Lil B

Dear Mother,
I love ya gurl!

From,

Jodi Arabia!

"You gotta live for yourself. Yourself and nobody else." —James Brown
↳ good inspiration if you want
to ever be a novelist. Screw college!

Johnny—

Things went bad last night. I'm shot. Give all my records to Roger and you get my rabbit, Cherokee. Tell Ma I love her and give her a kiss. I'm sorry things turned out like this but you know whatever. Love you,

—Mothra

17

SANTA to HITCHCOCK: MEMORIES.

by Santa Clause

Alfie and I didn't always get along well. I mean, how could I love him at first? He was just so naughty... But as time went on and I got to know him more and more, I really fell for the guy.

We were the best friends in the world. I'd always visit for the holidays; he'd come and help out at the workshop. Only God and myself know now all of the things we did together, and let me tell you — it's a surprise I haven't shown up on the naughty list once or twice.

With all joking aside, I'd like to tell you about Alfie's last breath — that haunting night I'll never forget, which has overshadowed all good memories. Whenever I think of Alfred now, all images of him are tainted by that last night...

...The phone rang very late that night. Alfred answered, not sounding too well. I knew I was in for something bad. In his last days, he grew too fat to touch his limbs to the floor, so he lived in a continuous slop.

"I'm naked," he told me. But I knew he was not. He wouldn't have been capable of disrobing in his state, but I knew he wished he were naked. I could hear him frantically fondling the Christmas tree beside him.

"Me too," I lied. I didn't want him to feel left out.

Then, Alfie began to cry.

"What's wrong, hun?" I asked.

"Santa," he pleaded, "I don't have much longer." I knew it. Somehow I knew it.

"Alfie, stay right where you are. Me and the missus are coming for you now."

"No. Not her. Besides, it'll be too late by the time you get here."

I reclined in my chair and began to weep. Why did he have to do this? Why my only friend?

"Alfred," I said. "I know I always tell you to wait till Christmas, but I'm making an exception tonight. I want you to open the present I gave you."

"Alright Santa."

I listened to Alfred struggle toward my gift. It was hard for him, but he made it. He began to open it; his weak fingers moved slowly. I heard him gasp at what it contained.

"Oh no. You didn't, Santa!" he exclaimed. I had gotten him silk underwear with our names stitched onto the butt. He always wanted a pair like it.

"Like them, ol' boy?" I weeped.

"Love them. Oh Santa... you'll always be ... on my naughty list."

"Promise... to check it twice ol' buddy."

"Santa?"

"Yes?"

"I love you," he told me.

"I love you more than you'll ever know naughty boy." And the line went dead. Alfie died. That was the end of Alfred Hitchcock...

ME
SANTA

WHAT A GR
LIFE
Teen Idols
LOL
Stop calling me Hitler!
IT is my WONDERFUL
ANNUAL B-DAY bash!
Bring some cash lol cuz I need to pay the rent
So join me, Charlachiz, in the exciting adventure we call life.
32011 West Blvd.
Little Rock, Arkansas 90000
(It will be the house with all the lizards)
Love,
CHARLACHIZ
JUNE 30
I wanna be an artist.

♡ wine ♡

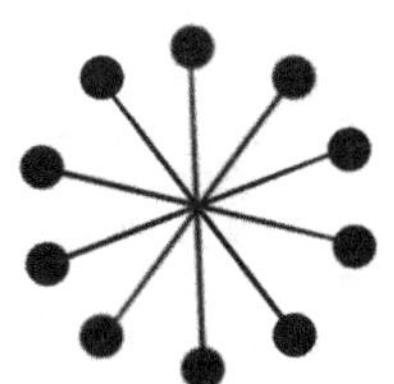

Ahh! I shit my pants!

n: a drink made out of grapes
that gets you drunk ♥

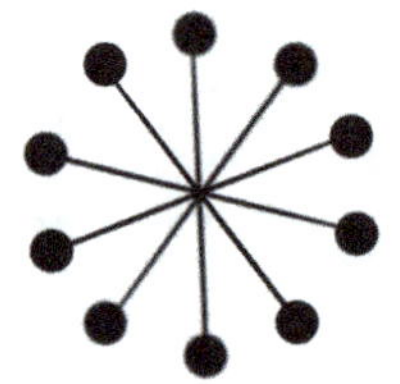

Gabe,

You don't have to apologize.
I slept with him too.

Call it even?

—Daddy

The Perp

Hey there. They call me the Perp. I come from Chicago in a part of town I like to call "Blues Alley". I'm what you'd call a coooool cat fiddlin' away my trombone. Coffee and cigarettes. Dollars and dames. Django Reinhart fills the air. I'm just a free bird, soaring my way through life. I chose the path of a blues man.

But not everything is perfect around here. Like that murder the other week. No good there. I just walked away from it.

<u>Mitch</u> / My dearest editor, is the Perp a good character? A good start to a NOVELLA?

— Syd

Mr. Rooter,

If you hum next time you are plumbing in my house, I will be forced to force you to wear my dog's shock collar.

Thank you for understanding.

−Ken

Dear Lindsey — LOVE O' MY LIFE,
First of all let me apologize for writing on such a small piece of paper even though I just bought <u>so much</u> new stationery, you cannot ever imagine. You know me, I don't like putting anything to waste so I'm using this! It just looked so pitiful sitting there all alone, just waiting for 'someone to pick it up and through it away. It knew death was around the corner but was not quite content with it yet. But I was it's savior. I hurried to the rescue and snatched it up in my iron grip and began scribbling away — giving this sad little scrap a life. I think that's what makes me such a good person. In some ways, I'm a better person than you because you would have went with the brand new stationery, I bet. Bitch Please.
  Well anyways, what I wanted to say in the first place is that I'm moving. It's only down the block so don't paniz. I just needed another room in my house. Two bedrooms are too little for a single man. I got a house with four. That way I can store my pinball machines and "Back to the Future" wax sculptures somewhere where they don't crowd my heart shaped jacuzzi and mock-time machine. Maybe you'll have a couch too for when you come over. You lucky girl you just might! Sorry it's just my bed issues... but you know about that.

Love,
The sad scrap savior,

Phil ♡ (I ♡ MYSELF)

So, what's the deal with that new kid, Jimmy?
—Arlene

DEAR SHANNON,
    YOU'RE SUCH A LOSER! JUST ENJOY THE SHOW. YOU KNOW, IT IS REALLY SAD HOW YOU'RE WORRYING YOUR LIFE AWAY. JUST STOP. RIGHT NOW. ~~THERE~~ THERE IS SO MUCH BEAUTY AROUND YOU. ALL YOU HAVE TO DO IS PAY ATTENTION. ONCE YOU GET THAT THROUGH YOUR FAT HEAD, WE CAN _ALL_ REJOICE! SHANNON, PLEASE LISTEN TO THIS ADVICE. I'M NOT JUST MAKING THIS UP. I WENT TO A TONY ROBBINS SEMINAR. IT ONLY MADE ME THINK OF YOU. PLEASE, JUST RECONSIDER HOW YOU VIEW LIFE SHANNON.
WITH _TOO_ MUCH LOVE,
       SABINA

Dear Roger,

Somehow, after all these years — all these fights — I still find myself madly, truley in love with you. I shouldn't forgive you; but I do. I forgive you wholely and completely. And since I forgive you for all of your indiscetions and fits of violence, I am now asking you to forgive me in return Roger. I did something ~~[scribbled]~~ horrible. I don't see how anyone can forgive what I've done, but I feel you owe it to me, Roger. Roger, it pains me to say this, but I... I did this certain awful thing... I shat myself... And not only did I do that, but I shat ~~[scribbled]~~ on top of your Grandmother. I'd like to say it was an accident, but I'd rather be honest. Love — *D.J.* *from Full House*

Please don't walk
out on us,
Sheryl.

-Wounded Heart (Me, Mike)

Oh what? This
isn't _sand
paper_?

Jennifer and Howard —
   Thank you so much for attending our wedding and making our day so special. Olive and I are so blessed to have friends like you in our lives. We love your gift, even though it wasn't on the registry (kidding!), because who doesn't love a good mixtape? We haven't listened to it yet, but we sure will on our road trip honeymoon. The track listing does seem rather monotonous, I have to admit. Is it just Billy Joe Royal's greatest hits with "White Wedding" by Billy Idol at the end? Was it a joke since my name is Billy? To be honest, if it was a joke, it was lost on both Olive and me. But it is appreciated none the less that you took the

time to put such a thing together.
I hope it plays, since it is
very scuffed up. Did you sit on
it by accident? Or is it just
old? I'm guessing it's just old
since it has someone else's name
on it. "To Holly" (Isn't that
Howard's ex???) Anyways, it's
a unique gift, like you both!

Thank you, and we
love you —
Olive and Billy

P.S. It would have been helpful
to provide a CD case with the
CD instead of putting it in a
jumbo Ziplock bag. Oh well,
next time.

Jazon!

Boy am I feeling spooky! I'll bet you look snazzy as Alfred Hitchcock tonight. I decided I'm going as Dolemite. If only you could be here with me on this night, Jazon. To watch the kids pass by. It brings many a tear to these tired eyes. If only, if only. Oh look at me! Jazon, you really bring out the tiny romantic man buried deep inside my soul. Whenever I think of you, Carl (that's the romantic man living inside of me) pops his head up to say hello. ~~Well~~ Well, more than hello, actually. More like, "Jazon, I crave your tender nipples"! Ha! Speaking of Carl, I need to get him a haircut... Well, anyways, enough about soul inhabiting midgets. Back to you, my sweet Jazon. Remember the night we first met? It was a few days before this fateful Hallows Eve. You were decorating the gym for the Halloween dance. It was real spooky. You're awfully talented Jazon. And remember how I got the wits scared straight out of me? Little Tommy Turner dangled that eerie toy spider in my face and I near peed my pants! But jeepers, was I glad you came to my rescue. ——— ———... ——— Sorry. I head to take a break. Calzones don't stay hot forever! As they say: time is warmth. Am I right? (Or 'write' since I'm little miss author over here, writing you a friggin' memoir! Look at me, how rude. This is by gosh the longest thing I've ever written. You're probably dying for it to be over ~~so~~ so you can get back to watching Jay Leno!) Anyways, I'm going out trick or treating. None of the girls could come out tonight so I guess it will just be me and the surrounding tykes. I love you Jazon. I cannot wait until we can trick 'n treat together! (We'll look pretty silly though, considering you're 45 and I'm 13.)

Love always, Prissy Princess

Fido 🦴

My boy. I am going to have to borrow your shock collar to put on my plumber. His humming is getting out of hand. I hope this doesn't cause too much trouble.

Your
owner,
Ven

22

Italian

1. greased back hair
2. rectangular glasses
3. budding mustache
4. arm hair
5. armpit hair
6. stains on clothing
7. father owns pizzeria
8. belly sticking out under shirt
9. tanktop
10. cargo shorts
11. leg hair
12. socks with sandals
13. open-toe Keen* knock-offs
14. fat
15. sweaty
16. short
17. happy & enthusiastic toward strangers

Mama Mia!

*or any major sandal brand

Proto-TYKE!

Salvador!
You are the
WORST
gardner I've ever hired
— EVER!
Don't EVEN take out
the trash! I'll do it
MYSELF!!! Fuck the
hedges too — I'll trim
them!
— Gen

Chuck Palanuk's
~~Parker & Kansas~~ ~~Diary!~~

Introduction

So. You probably wanna hear a story about some fairy tale wedding and a knight in shining armor. Well, news flash! This book is gritty. It's dirty. It's grimy. Therefore don't even bother if you like all that Disney crap. Selena Gomez? Please. Miley Cyrus? Who? Sarah Jessica Parker? You mean that whiny bitch from Sex and the City? Puh-lease! Come on girlfriend. You know I don't like all of that Donald Duck & Mickey Mouse shit. And I never even set foot near anything designer, or any of that fancy smancy bull-SHIZ! I'm violent. I'm gross. I'm... I'm... the ultimate tom boy.

Ch. 1

Chuck Palaniuk
(author)

So you know all those little boys who are into dump trucks and dirt and ooey-gooey-sticky things? Well then, I guess you could have ~~____~~ called me a little boy. Growing up, I never befriended those little tea party yuppies. ~~________~~ [Pause] I know what you're thinking. This girl reminds me of my five year old bro. Well, if you're grossed out now you just wait. It doesn't get any better than this. Only down hill from here. Note to reader: Enjoy the ride!

[RESUME]

This little Chap-Chap (Chapter for you idiots out there who don't understand chelo speak) is going to be about one of those witty little anecdots that your parents tell your new boy-toy that you bring home and you get all embarresed. Cheeks turn red. Then you begin to salvate when your mom brings out the peach cobbler. And not just because you want cobbler. Its like you became rabid! And trust me. It is not just because of the cobbler!

Anyways, let me get back to this wit-fest. "Mom! Bring out the baby booooook! My boy-toy wants to hear the story where I almost killed little Henry Vargas!" Hold the onions. I don't want this story STINKING! (and by the way, my boy-toy is no boy at all. He has werewolf running through his veins.

I know it.)
"This is such a cute story,"
my mom says.
"Mom. I ordered this with
sugar-coating on side, cuz this
ain't sweet. You better watch out
Jason. You'll get a whole world
of wow-oh-my-god-she-did-that-
wow-oh-my-god-I'm-dating-her.
in your cute little werewolf face."
Then my mom had to make
some comment on how "smart"
I am. Oooooo. I know big words.
BIG DEAL. Doesn't she know
I'm failing all of my classes
including the easy-as-pie little
weenie-for-brain ones? Jeez, Get a
life mom. Don't waste your time
worshiping an idiot a.k.a. me.
So the story begins. When I was
just seven years of age (I know. I
talk all Shakespearean) I met a

cute little brat who just happened to be male. (I don't pick friends off ~~[illegible]~~ of gender. That goes to show you that I was never one of those "ew-cooties cooties" types of girl. TOMBOY ALERT!). This boy's name was Henry Vargas. Naturally I called him Var-gassy-Ass! I was the little shit in town! Throwing my wit all around! (how very Dr. Suess of me)

One day, Var-gassy-ass brought a little jizzy boy to school. And you know how kids are all over juice boxes like Jazons over me. And lets just say a certain someone wouldn't share their juicebox with another certain someone and it made that certain someone certainly angry so that other certain someone certainly got stabbed with the straw ~~[illegible]~~ from his juice box in his fucking eye! I didn't get in trouble. Simply self-defence. He did try to hit me. Right?

Uh-oh. I smell cobbler. I think it's berry. Get out the whipped cream, mom. This certain someone is hungry.

[Ch. 2] THE BIG BANG

In my not so chronological lifestory, we will go all over the place. Like crapping in chemistry one day to lunching in the library in another. It's like Sixteen Candles. Actually, more like Sixteen Black Candles Used for Black Magic. Or it's like Say Anything. More like say Nothing cause you'll be at a loss for words. (Footnote: Little People Big World? More like Big People Little World since you're always bumping into people.) (continued on page 189)

Mortal Being #368115F2:
Cassandra Court

It is time for me to collect your soul. Have it ready for me by

6:55 AM

My pleasure—

the Devil 666

DEAR JACOB,
I WILL BE LEAVING TONIGHT AT 12:00 AM. I WILL NOT BE SEEING YOU ANYMORE. I AM SO SORRY. I FEEL TERRIBLE BUT I JUST CANNOT DO THIS ANY LONGER. WHY DO YOU HAVE TO LIKE THE MOVIE SHAMPOO? IT'S TERRIBLE! WITH THOSE ACTORS, I MEAN, IT HAD POTENTIAL BUT WOW! IT WAS REALLY THAT BAD! JACOB, I AM NOT TELLING YOU WHERE I AM GOING AND I AM TAKING YOUR TEDDY-BEAR SHIRT WITH ME. I'M SORRY.   —LORI

(866) 908-5220

(877) 908-5220

5582 McFadden Avenue
Huntington Beach, CA 92649

175 S. Lake Avenue #200
Pasadena, CA 91101

P.S.
I WISH I

ED YOU

Please, with all
do respect.

Bitch
Please

Love
your mother,
angie

MY SUICIDE NOTE!

Life is so cruel. I am so sorry to do this to all of you, but ever since I saw the movie "The Naked Babie's Hand" I knew that humanity ~~was~~ is doomed, and I cannot stay around to face the end. I am not brave enough. I'm so sorry to all of those ~~morning~~ mourning me. I have one word of advice to everybody living ~~on~~ on this planet. Do ~~not~~ see "The Naked Babie's Hand." If you do, you will ~~me~~ most likely meet the same fate as I, as doomed as humanity, and soon as I dead as disco.

Sincerely,

Margo Ann Marie Scratchy Larrise
and
Evelyn Grace Florence Ann Larrise

(We are ~~siamese~~ siamese.)

S. O. S.

Thanks for picking up this bottle. I'm forced to carve these letters with a stick so I won't write too much. But, well, just can you please, well—

HELP ME?

I'm stuck on an island and I am staaaaarved to death if I ever heard of it. Send me a copter or something.

—Squig

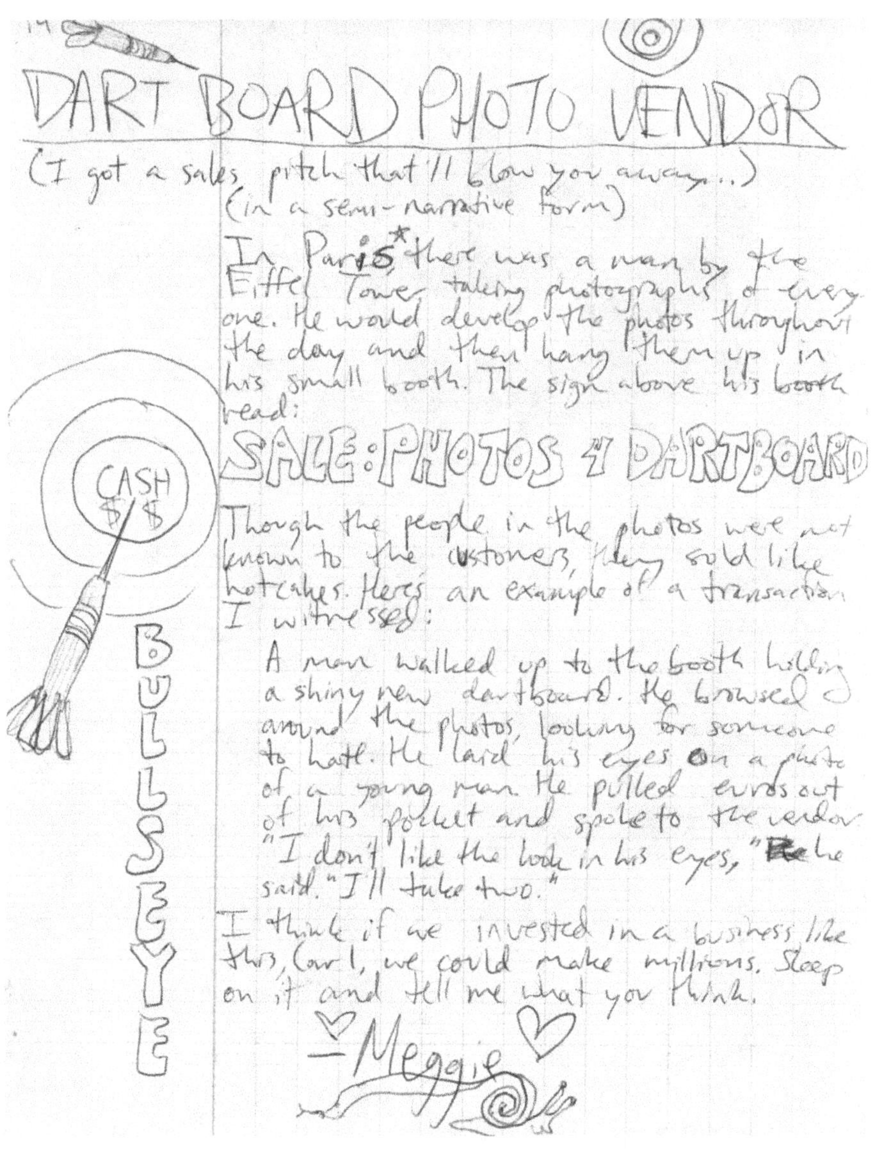

DART BOARD PHOTO VENDOR

(I got a sales pitch that'll blow you away...)
(in a semi-narrative form)

In Paris*, there was a man by the Eiffel Tower taking photographs of everyone. He would develop the photos throughout the day and then hang them up in his small booth. The sign above his booth read:

SALE: PHOTOS 4 DARTBOARD

Though the people in the photos were not known to the customers, they sold like hotcakes. Here's an example of a transaction I witnessed:

A man walked up to the booth holding a shiny new dartboard. He browsed around the photos, looking for someone to hate. He laid his eyes on a photo of a young man. He pulled euros out of his pocket and spoke to the vendor. "I don't like the look in his eyes," he said. "I'll take two."

I think if we invested in a business like this, Carl, we could make millions. Sleep on it and tell me what you think.

♡ —Meggie ♡

FOR
SALE
I ♥ PARIS

A in the U.K.!

Love,
Angie &
Lydia ♡ A ⊙

Hey, I'm
the new
girl in
town. ♡

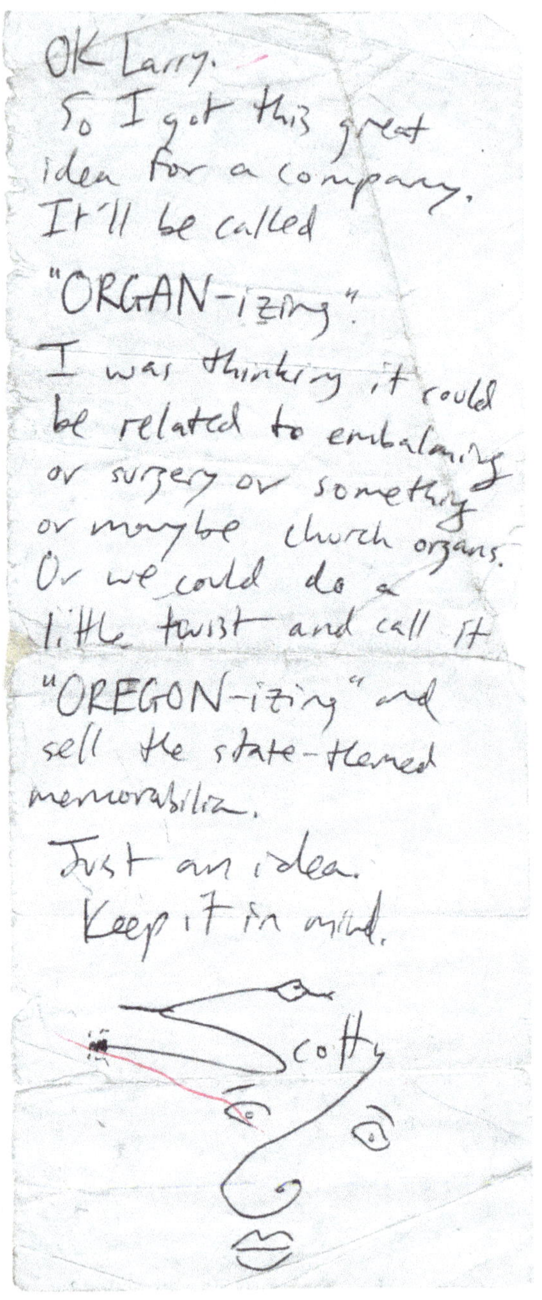

OK Larry.
So I got this great
idea for a company.
It'll be called

"ORGAN-izing".
I was thinking it could
be related to embalming
or surgery or something
or maybe church organs.
Or we could do a
little twist and call it

"OREGON-izing" and
sell the state-themed
memorabilia.

Just an idea.
Keep it in mind.

Scotty

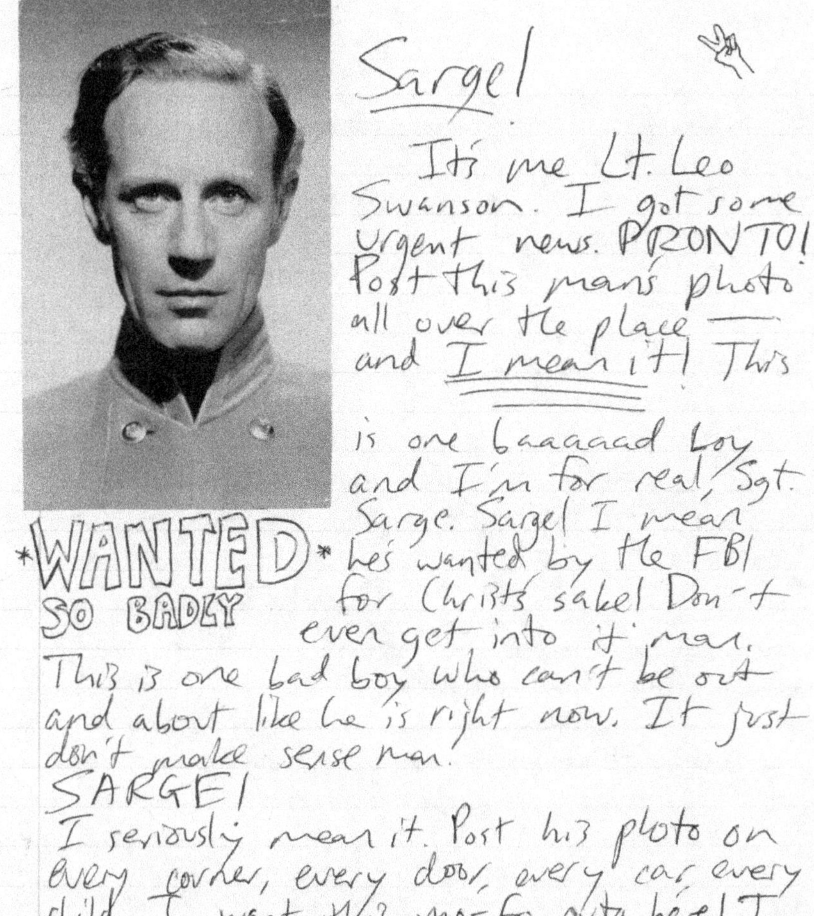

Sarge!
It's me Lt. Leo Swanson. I got some urgent news. PRONTO! Post this man's photo all over the place — and <u>I mean it!</u> This

is one baaaaad boy and I'm for real, Sgt. Sarge. Sarge I mean he's wanted by the FBI for Christ's sake! Don't even get into it man.
This is one bad boy who can't be out and about like he is right now. It just don't make sense man.
SARGE!
I seriously mean it. Post his photo on every corner, every door, every car every child. I want this mo-fo outa here! I don't even like thinkin' 'bout all the bad things he did. Sarge! POST THIS PHOTO EVERYWHERE. I want him arrested, then prisoned, then lethal injected!
 —Lt. Leo Swanson

Peeves!
You are the WORST butler... EVER! ~~First~~, you don't take out the trash. Then, you dont respond to the bell when I ring for you!!! JUST FORGET IT! I-ll ~~scrub~~ my OWN goddam ~~back~~!!! Last time I ever trust a butler with anything important!!
— BEN BEN

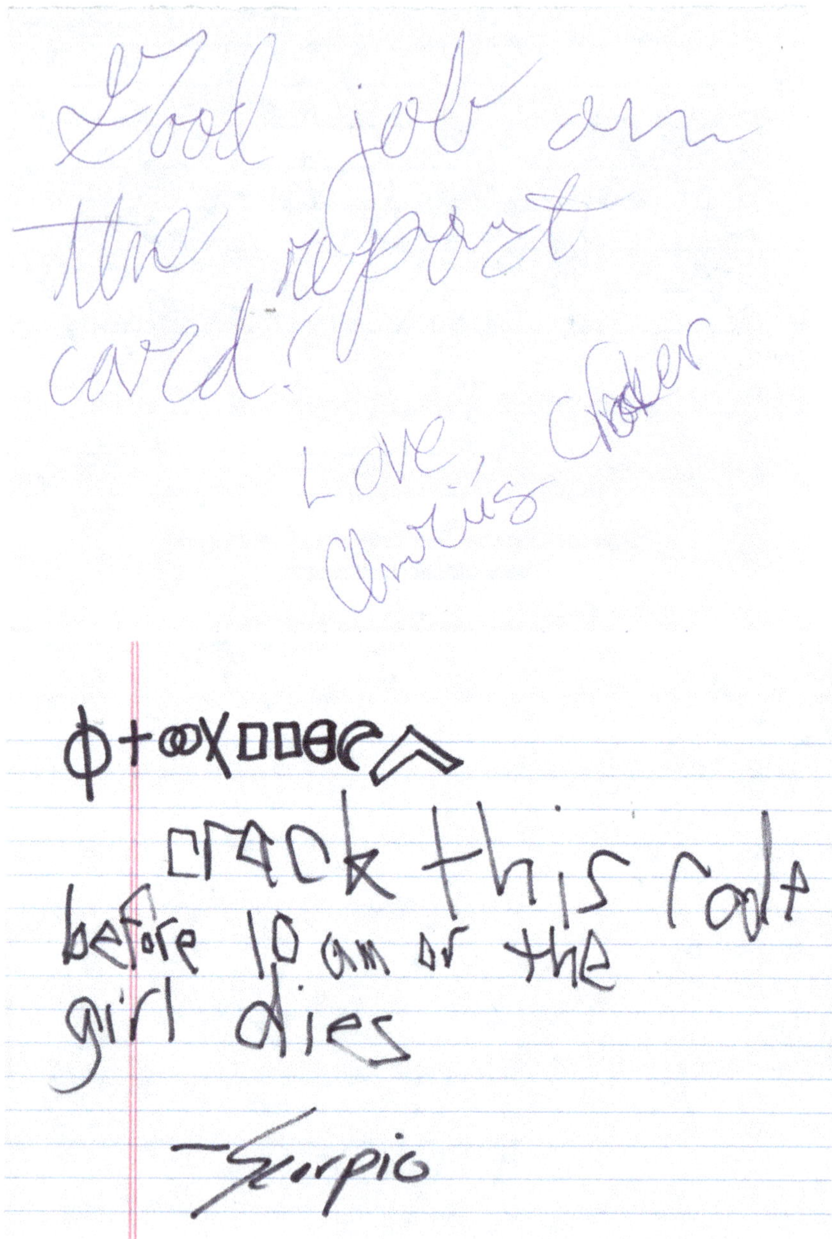
Good job on
the report
card!

Love,
Chains Choker

⌀†∞✕▢▢▣☖⌂
⊏⊓⍺⊏k this code
before 10 am or the
girl dies

—Scorpio

Nancy,

I long for your lips.

PUCKER UP

— Mr. Big

39645NP

Hay!!we are going to get along just swell.

LOVE LOVE LOVE
ALWAYS!

rachelle

"Superior Customer Service Without Compromise"
www.usanationaltitle.com

the teachers will never catch us passing notes

National Title Company

(866) 908-5220

(877) 908-5220

5582 McFadden Avenue
Huntington Beach, CA 92649

175 S. Lake Avenue #200
Pasadena, CA 91101

Mommy loves you so so much. I'll miss you.

Your mother,

Angie.

Dada,
Mama
said there'd
be days like
this.

—Shinelle

Hey!
Napoleon Dynamite is
on at 7. Do you
want to join me?
— Arlene

fuck
me

Six months.
It's been six fucking
months.

— Sheriff
Hot Dog

Stop talking to me.

— Haruki Murakami

WANTED

Hello. My name is DJ Puppy Dog Face. I have new hip hop single "Lick My Bowl Clean" but I need to record dogs barking. If you have dog or you sound like dog. Hit me up. No pay, sorry. I'll provide subway/dog food (depending on talent).

dogtearz69@aol.com

Keep your values positive
because your values will
become your future.
Starting from   now!

Sorry, but I used your
HW as a pad.

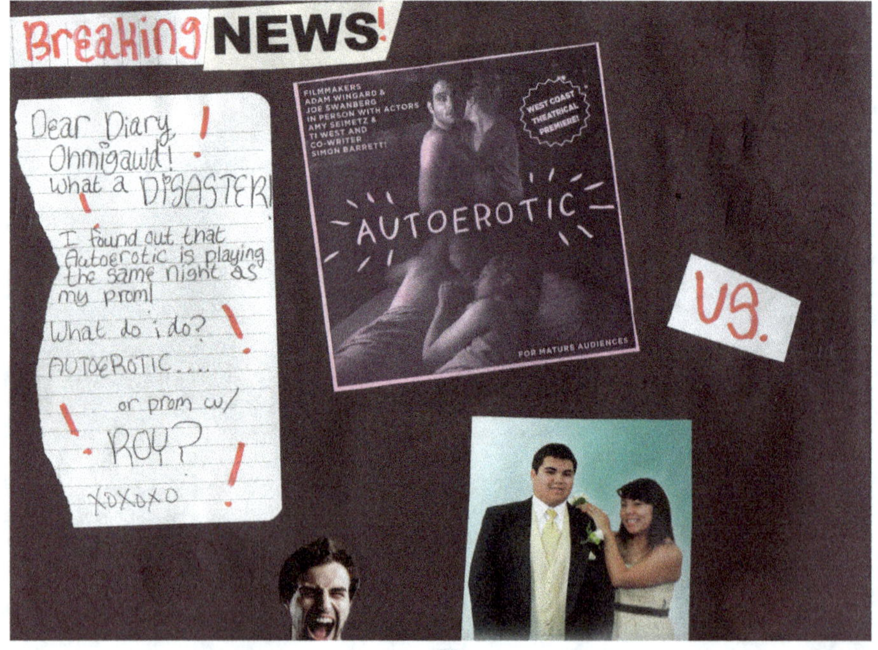

About the Authors

Kansas Bowling is a writer and filmmaker living in Nevada. Her first book from Far West is about her second feature film *Cuddly Toys*. It is titled *A Cuddly Toys Companion*. When she is not writing or working on films, Kansas is busy prospecting at her desert lode mine and being a custodian of the Mojave Desert. She is the proud owner of the Old Glory Theatre in Hawthorne, Nevada. (Open soon!) She is also an amateur detective and the #1 fan of C.W. McCall.

Parker Love Bowling is an actress, writer and filmmaker from Los Angeles, California. Her debut poetry collection, *Rhododendron, Rhododendron*, comes out in 2022 via Far West Press.

About the Illustrator

Elizabeth Zamets is a Los Angeles based artist and editorial illustrator curious about all things tender, seemingly insignificant, and strange. She has a BFA from Otis College of Art and Design in Illustration.

Also Out On Far West

SONNY VINCENT......................................Snake Pit Therapy

BRENT L. SMITH....................................Pipe Dreams on Pico

JOSEPH MATICK......................................The Baba Books

KURT EISENLOHR....................................Stab the Remote

KANSAS BOWLING..............A Cuddly Toys Companion

JENNIFER ROBIN..........You Only Bend Once with a Spoonful of Mercury

PARKER LOVE BOWLING................Rhododendron, Rhododendron

CRAIG DYER..........Heavier Than A Death in the Family

farwestpress.com